What's the Weather?

IT'S SNOWING!

By Alex Appleby

Gareth Stevens
Publishing

Please visit our website, www.garethstevens.com. For a free color catalog of all our high-quality books, call toll free 1-800-542-2595 or fax 1-877-542-2596.

Library of Congress Cataloging-in-Publication Data

Appleby, Alex.
It's snowing! / by Alex Appleby.
    p. cm. — (What's the weather)
Includes index.
ISBN 978-1-4339-9401-2 (pbk.)
ISBN 978-1-4339-9402-9 (6-pack)
ISBN 978-1-4339-9400-5 (library binding)
1. Snow —Juvenile literature. 2. Weather — Juvenile literature. I. Appleby, Alex. II. Title.
QC926.37 A66 2014
551.5784—dc23

First Edition

Published in 2014 by
Gareth Stevens Publishing
111 East 14th Street, Suite 349
New York, NY 10003

Copyright © 2014 Gareth Stevens Publishing

Editor: Ryan Nagelhout
Designer: Andrea Davison-Bartolotta

All illustration by Michael Harmon

Printed in the United States of America

CPSIA compliance information: Batch #CS13GS: For further information contact Gareth Stevens, New York, New York at 1-800-542-2595.

Contents

It is cold outside.

Big dark clouds fill the sky.

7

It starts to snow outside!

I put on a heavy
green jacket.
It keeps me warm.

I wear blue
gloves outside.

No two snowflakes
are alike.

I move the snow
with a shovel.

17

I roll the snow
into a snowball.

19

Three big snowballs make a snowman.

I put a red hat on it.

23

Words to Know

shovel

snowball

snowman

Index